© 1999 Landoll, Inc.
Ashland, Ohio 44805
® The Landoll Apple Logo is a trademark owned by Landoll, Inc.
and is registered with the U.S. Patent and Trademark Office.
No part of this book may be reproduced or copied.
All Rights Reserved. Made in China.

00514-1287

by
Patricia Wilson

Billy Bunny raced past the Bunny Bunch house, waving a piece of paper in his hand and shouting, "Big bike parade on Friday! The best decorated bike wins a shiny new Blue Streak bike!"

Early the next morning, Brother Bunny got out his red bike. He found a small flag and some streamers left over from the Fourth of July. Then he washed and polished his bike till it was shiny enough to see his face in it.

Sister Bunny dug through all of Mother's sewing baskets and found lots of pink, lavender and yellow ribbons, bows and buttons. She didn't need to wash her bike, because she never rode it in the mud.

Meanwhile, Grandpa had disappeared into the tool shed. He had the door closed with a sign on it that said, "Do Not Disturb!" After hearing the hammering and sawing, Brother and Sister tried to peek into the shed.

"What's he doing?" asked Sister.

"I'm not sure," said Brother. "Just making noise, I think."

When Father Bunny came home, Sister Bunny met him at the driveway with her pink bike all decorated. Bows were tied to every place possible to hang a bow! And if there wasn't a bow, a ribbon dangled with big buttons on the end of it.

"You sure look pretty on that pink bike." Father smiled at Sister Bunny. "And your bike is pretty, too!"

Just then, Brother Bunny rode into view. His bike was covered with streamers and red, white and blue ribbons. A silver sparkler decorated each handle grip. "Hey, Father! Look at my bike!" shouted Brother Bunny.

And just when Father Bunny thought he had seen it all, out of the tool shed came Grandpa riding his old bicycle! He'd attached a silver bucket to the handle bars, and hooked a large umbrella to the back of the seat. But best of all, on each side, Grandpa had attached a wheelbarrow with seats for passengers!

"Wow, Grandpa!" said Sister Bunny. "Take us for a ride!"

"Please, Grandpa! Wait for us!" called Brother Bunny.

Mother Bunny and Grandma Bunny came out of the house to see what was happening.

"You aren't planning on riding that in the parade?" asked Father Bunny.

"I have to if I want to win that Blue Streak," said Grandpa.

Everyone laughed.

At the parade the next day, Brother Bunny and Sister Bunny were happy to cheer for Grandpa Bunny as he rode his new bike down the main street. All the bunnies laughed and pointed at Grandpa Bunny, but they all secretly wanted to take a ride.

And guess what! Grandpa Bunny's crazy contraption won the bike contest and the new Blue Streak—for being the silliest bike in the parade!

That day, and on many others, Grandpa stayed busy giving rides to the Bunny Bunch and to anyone else who asked. It was Grandpa's greatest surprise!